Achieving a Dream

by Jill Atkins and Alessia Trunfio

W
FRANKLIN WATTS
LONDON • SYDNEY

Achieving a Dream

Contents

Chapter 1	Where am I?	4
Chapter 2	Beginning to Remember	8
Chapter 3	I Can Ride	12
Chapter 4	What a Nightmare	15
Chapter 5	Bad News, Good News	19
Chapter 6	Down in the Dumps	22
Chapter 7	Max's Challenge	25
Chapter 8	The Sky's the Limit	27

Chapter 1
Where am I?

I opened my eyes and blinked in the brightness, unable to understand what I was seeing: white above, and blue, green and white surrounding me. Closing my eyes, I tried to think. *What's happening? Where am I?* **Who** *am I? Could this be a weird dream?*

Calm down, I told myself. I concentrated on taking deep breaths. *There must be an explanation.* One thing I knew for certain: I was lying on my back. But why?

I listened. *Bleep, bleep, bleep* ... came from somewhere to the right of my head.

Tip, tap, tip, tap ... that must be footsteps, coming closer.

Swish ... a curtain was drawn aside to my left. I sensed movement nearby.

I opened my eyes again and looked up. Someone was leaning over me: a young man with black hair and a beard. "Hello," he said with a smile. "So you decided to return to us? Welcome back!"

I frowned. *Why did he say that?* I couldn't remember having gone anywhere. *Who are you?* I wanted to ask, but I found I couldn't speak.

"I'm Krish," said the young man, as if he had heard my question. "I'm your nurse. I'm here to look after you. You're in hospital," explained Krish. "You've been here a couple of days. You're concussed. You've been unconscious and you have a badly broken leg."

Only then did I become aware of the pain. My left leg was throbbing and for the first time, I noticed the raised hump towards the end of the bed where my legs were.

"That's a kind of cage," said Krish. "It takes the weight of the bed covers off your broken leg."

I stared at the raised covers. Everything was so confusing.

"Your mum's here," said Krish. I turned my head.

"Ruby, darling!"

Ruby! So that's my name. And this pretty, dark-haired woman is my mum.

"We've been so worried," she said, tears in her eyes.

I felt my eyes watering too. "Mum?" I murmured. My voice was croaky, my throat dry.

"Now, don't upset yourself," said Krish. "You just need to rest. You'll be back to your old self in no time."

He walked around the bed and spoke softly to Mum.

"Ruby seems to have some memory loss," he whispered.

"Try not to worry. It should come back eventually, but be prepared for Ruby not remembering some things for a while."

He turned to me, not realising I'd heard what he had said.

"I'll leave you two to chat," he said. "Call me if you need me." He winked at me then turned away, closing the curtain and walking away down the corridor.

"Oh, Ruby, love," said Mum. "You've had such a nasty knock. You frightened the life out of all of us."

"How? What did ...?"

"You probably don't remember. You fell at the skate park."

"Skate park?" What was Mum talking about? I didn't have a skateboard, although I'd wanted one for ages.

"You were practising one of your daredevil stunts," Mum explained. "You landed awkwardly, and knocked yourself out."

I shook my head crossly, starting to cry again. "But, Mum, you *know* I haven't saved enough for a skateboard yet!"

"Ruby, you must have forgotten. You bought it with your birthday money."

I squeezed my eyes shut and tried to remember.

Chapter 2
Beginning to Remember

I'm going into The Skate Shack with Dad and my friend, Max.

The skateboards are lined up on the high shelf. I'm so excited!

It's been my dream to have a board since I was seven.

Max helps me choose the best one. It's yellow with

red speed stripes down the middle. I've got just enough money.

"Oh, yes," I said to Mum. "I remember that now, but I haven't had a chance to use it yet."

"Of course you have. You, Max and Agata ..." Mum stopped mid-sentence, seeing the tears pouring down my face.

"I can't remember, Mum," I sobbed.

"Hush. Don't worry, sweetheart." Mum reached over and held my hand. "I think it's time you had another sleep. I'll go and get a coffee and ring Dad. He'll be here as soon as he finishes work."

Sure enough, the next time I opened my eyes, Dad was sitting there.

"Hi," he said, kissing my forehead. "Thank goodness you've come round. I've been going mad with worry!"

I smiled at Dad. "I'm fine now," I said, trying to reassure

him. But my smile faded as he spoke ...

"Mum says you can't remember using your board," he said.

"I'm amazed. You've spent so much time on it lately,

experimenting with twists and turns, and ..."

"Why do you and Mum keep insisting I used the board?"

I shouted. "I *didn't*. I couldn't have done!"

"Let's change the subject, shall we?" Dad suggested.

"How about our holiday? Where do you fancy going?"

The time passed quickly. We both enjoyed thinking and

talking about the exciting places we might go. Eventually,

Dad had to leave. "Get some more sleep," he said as

he gave me a hug. "I'll pop in tomorrow before work."

When Dad had gone, I lay alone and tried to remember.

Mum and Dad insisted I had used my new board, but my memory was completely blank. I decided to ask if Max and Agata could visit me soon. They would tell me the truth. It was not that I disbelieved Mum or Dad, but I just couldn't understand why I couldn't recall anything. It was all very worrying.

Perhaps, I thought, if I shut my eyes again and concentrated hard, I might remember a bit more.

I'm on the front drive with Agata and Max. I'm trying out my skateboard for the very first time. I'm dead nervous. I watch carefully what the others do. They are so skilled and well-balanced on theirs, I think skating must be easy, but I'm so wobbly that I keep falling off, time and again. In the end we are all laughing so much that I think it's time to give up for the day.

So it was true! I *had* tried out my skateboard!

Chapter 3
I Can Ride

Now I began to think about what Mum and Dad

had told me. It seemed more and more likely that I'd had

a bang on the head. That would explain my memory loss.

I tried to sit up, but had to flop back onto the pillows.

I felt totally weak. And I was really thirsty. So I pressed

the little button I found next to the bed.

Krish came hurrying over. "What is it?" he asked,

pouring me a glass of water.

"If you lose your memory, does it come back?"

"Usually, yes," Krish answered. "Why do you ask?"

"Well, I heard what you said to Mum and ..."

"You agree your memory is limited right now?"

"Yeah. Mum and Dad say that I had a skateboard accident.

I don't remember it, but I keep getting flashbacks."

"Don't worry. That's quite normal," Krish reassured me.

"I expect you'll remember more as time goes on.

Now, settle down. It's time for you to get some sleep."

But try as I might, I couldn't doze off. I couldn't help

wondering what else I might be able to remember.

I hoped that, eventually, my entire memory would return.

Just as I thought I might actually fall asleep ...

I'm at the skate park with Agata and Max and some others.

They're all so experienced at skateboarding. I try to copy

their tricks and fall off several times, but I'm learning.

It's fantastic fun and I don't mind a few knocks.

I smiled to myself and sat up. "So, I definitely rode my board,"
I said quietly. "And I did fall off many times. But when did I
really hurt myself? Think, Ruby, think!"
I closed my eyes tight and willed myself to remember.

*I'm really good at this. My legs are strong. I'm a bit of
a daredevil and it feels ace, zooming up and down the ramps,
twisting and turning, leaping in somersaults. Flying through
the air feels great. Wow! I hope my friends are impressed by
how much I've improved. I've just got time for one more stunt.
Here I go! Ahh! I'm falling ... falling ... falling ...*

Now my memory was coming back, big time. I couldn't
imagine how I'd ever sleep after that. I wanted to leap in
the air and tell the world: "I can ride a skateboard!" But, no.
I was stuck in bed with a broken leg and a concussion.
It seemed ages before I eventually drifted off to sleep.

14

Chapter 4

What a Nightmare

It's the day of the Inter-school Athletics Championships.

I can't remember why I'm there, but I'm at the track with Agata.

My coach, Mr Holloway, is with us. Suddenly, the scene changes.

There's a high pole ahead of me. I run and try to jump, but

my legs are like lead. I'm stuck there. I try to get off the ground

again and again, but it's no good. I can't do it ... I can't jump ...

"Help!" I cry ...

I woke up shivering.

"You shouted," said Krish, leaning over to feel my forehead.

"You OK?"

"Not really. I had a nightmare. It was horrible." I bit my lip.

It was almost impossible to say it out loud. "I couldn't jump.

And that's what I've always done – jump."

"Jump how? Long jump? High jump?" asked Krish.

"High jump. How could I have forgotten that?"

"You're good, eh?"

"I guess so. I was supposed to try out for the county team

next week, only now I can't because ..."

"You've gone and broken your leg!"

I felt too embarrassed to tell Krish of my ambitions.

He would think I was boasting, but it was my dream

one day to be World Champion, Olympic gold medallist.

Just then, I heard two voices I recognised: Agata and Max.

Krish went to meet them.

"Hello," he said. "You must be Ruby's friends. Her mum told me about you two. Welcome to the ward. Come on in, but don't stay too long. You mustn't tire her. She's had a nasty bang on the head."

Agata and Max came rushing to my bedside. Agata leaned over and hugged me. Max stared at the protective cage around my leg.

"Wow! That's awesome," he said with a mischievous grin. "Are you OK now? Everyone wants to know how you are."

I nodded, but I didn't feel OK. "Did my parents tell you I seem to have lost my memory?"

"Yeah," said Agata. "That's so weird."

"Well, I've been gradually getting it back. I think I remember my accident at the skate park now."

"I couldn't look," admitted Max.

"Only, last night I had a nightmare." I paused. It was awkward trying to explain without bursting into tears, something I wanted to avoid in front of my friends. "And that made me remember the high jump. I had completely forgotten. The championships ... I think I'm going to miss them."

"What a nightmare!" groaned Max.

Chapter 5
Bad News, Good News

Next morning, Mum arrived in time for the doctor's visit.

"I'm Dr Cameron," the doctor said, shaking hands with me.

"I operated on your leg. I've come to give you an update."

She removed the bed clothes and the protective cage.

I stared down at my legs, the left one encased in

white plaster.

"How bad is it?" asked Mum.

"Well," explained Dr Cameron, "it was quite a bad break.

Ruby fractured the tibia
and fibula – the two bones
below the knee – right at
the bottom above the ankle."

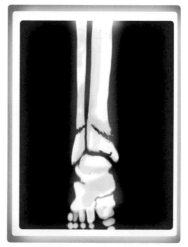

"Will it take very long to heal?" Mum asked.

"Usually about six weeks for the bones to knit together."

"Oh," I mumbled, frowning. That was definitely the end of my hopes in the County Championships.

Mum squeezed my hand. "There'll be another chance to achieve your dream," she whispered.

The doctor looked at me and raised her eyebrows. "Is there a special reason you're anxious for a full recovery?"

"She's an amazing high jumper," said Mum.

"Ah. That's great to hear," said Dr Cameron with a smile. "How high can you jump?"

"One metre forty," I said.

"Wow! That sounds brilliant," she said. "So I guess you've got ambitions?"

"Yeah. County Championships are next month."

"I'm really sorry, but I'm afraid you're going to have to miss them."

I bit my lip. How I wished I hadn't been so reckless at the skate park!

"So is there any good news?" I sighed. "Will I be able to jump again?"

"Of course," said Dr Cameron. "You'll need lots of physiotherapy after the plaster comes off and you'll need to be patient and work hard. Then, if you stick to your exercises, I've no doubt that you'll make a full recovery. I shall expect to hear your name as a successful athlete in the future!"

I tried to smile at Dr Cameron, but it was impossible. Six weeks in plaster? It was an unbearable length of time to wait before my leg would be recovered enough to compete. My left leg was my take-off leg. I needed it to be strong and flexible. Getting it well enough for the competition was going to be an uphill struggle.

Chapter 6
Down in the Dumps

The next day, Krish helped me to get out of bed and walk with crutches, and although he was kind and positive, I couldn't bring myself to be cheerful. I felt totally miserable and frustrated. I kept thinking about how I should be on the field, practising and improving my approach. I still couldn't believe I wasn't going to be able to compete.

When my friends visited again that afternoon, I wasn't in the mood for chatting. They left after only a few minutes. Max complained that I wasn't like the Ruby he knew. "Of course I'm not!" I snapped. "Nor would you be if you had to put up with this."

"Time for physio," announced Krish, arriving at my bedside

a bit later. "Come with me."

Frowning at the pain in my leg, I struggled along

the hospital corridors. Krish left me at a large hall kitted

out with all kinds of gym equipment.

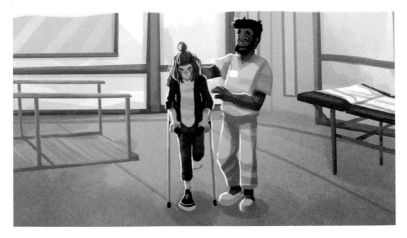

"Hi, Ruby. I'm Emma," said a tall young woman. "I want

to check how you're getting on and give you some

exercises you can do when you get home."

"OK." I didn't feel very enthusiastic about the exercises.

All I really wanted to do was lie in bed, bury myself under

the covers and pretend none of this was happening.

Half an hour later, I didn't feel any better. Emma had tried to cheer me up with a few jokes, but I didn't feel like smiling. Then, just as I was about to leave the gym and head back to the ward, I saw a boy in a wheelchair. He was laughing with his trainer as he performed muscle-strengthening exercises with his arms.

"That's a future 10,000 metre wheelchair champion, if ever I saw one," said Emma. "He's lovely. Such a positive attitude."

That made me think. Perhaps I wasn't so badly off, after all.

Chapter 7
Max's Challenge

The next time, when Max and Agata came to visit,

they brought a draughts board and some books.

"We thought you might like to take your mind off things,"

said Agata.

I laughed. "You mean you thought I was in such misery,

you'd better try and cheer me up?"

"Looks like you've done a bit of that yourself," said Max

with a smile.

"Yeah, well, I've been thinking," I said.

"Hey, don't overdo it! You've had a concussion, you know!"

he teased.

"I'm OK. Things aren't so bad. And I think I might be going

home in a couple of days."

"Mr Holloway's been asking about you," Agata told me.

"Thanks, though he won't be interested if I can't compete."

"No, you're wrong," said Agata. "He's really keen to get you back into training. Of course, you'll miss this round of championships, but there's always the indoor athletics in the winter."

"That's true," I agreed. "Thanks, Agata. I'll get fit for that."

"Mr Holloway has *high* hopes for you," she said, and we all laughed at her bad joke.

"That can be your challenge," said Max. "Six weeks in plaster then a few more weeks training and getting absolutely fit. But first, I challenge you to a game of draughts."

Two days later, Krish found me in the day room, immersed in a book. I looked up when I heard him approach.

"I've got some good news," he said with a smile. "I'll be sorry to lose you, but you're going home tomorrow."

Chapter 8
The Sky's the Limit

The next six weeks passed slowly for me. The X-rays
showed that my bones were healing well. I concentrated on
doing the exercises Emma had given me to do, but I was
still really fed up with the time it was taking.

Mr Holloway visited me at home. "Let me know when
you're ready to come back into training, Ruby," he said.

"Can't wait!" I said. "I've been looking at reports
from the Schools' Track and Field Championships.
There have been new records set all over the place."

"Not in the high jump. That record is waiting for you!"
I laughed. "Max issued me with a challenge," I said.
"I'm hoping to compete in the Junior Indoor
Championships in December."

Mr Holloway looked doubtful.

"Well, that would be great," he said, "but are you sure you'll be fit by then?"

"Definitely! I'm aiming high! I'm determined to achieve my dream. This is where I start."

At last the six weeks were up. When the plaster was removed, I stared, horrified, at my pale, thin leg. I could have cried.

"Don't look so worried," said the doctor. "It's quite normal. A few exercises will bring it back to looking like the other leg."

I limped at first, but as soon as the serious training began, the limp improved quickly and soon vanished. After school and at the athletics club, I started with gentle jogging, then running and eventually — low at first — the high jump. The bar was raised one notch at a time.

The day of the Indoor Championships arrived. After all my preparations, would my leg hold up? I looked over at Mr Holloway. He gave me the thumbs up.

"Go for it!" he said, smiling. "The sky's the limit!"

"I can't jump quite that high," I laughed, "but I'll try."

Maybe, just maybe, my dream of becoming Olympic and World Champion was achievable after all!

Things to think about

1. How did Ruby feel when she first woke up?
2. What scene came to Ruby in her first flashback? What clues in the book tell you it's a flashback?
3. What discouraging information did Dr Cameron give to Ruby? How did Ruby's mood change after this?
4. What inspiring scene helped Ruby begin to change her mind about her fate?
5. What steps did Ruby take to be sure she would recover well? Do you think she can reach her goals?

Write it yourself

This book describes a serious injury experienced by a young athlete, and explores her road to recovery. Now try to write your own story about hard work in the face of tragedy. Think about the obstacles your main characters will face, and what helps them find the courage to continue. Plan your story before you begin to write it. Start off with a story map:

- a beginning to introduce the characters and where and when your story is set (the setting);
- a problem that the main characters will need to fix in the story;
- an ending where the problems are resolved.

Get writing! Try to include a varied timeline so readers get a sense of the back story, which creates drama.

How would the dialogue change to express a change in mood or perspective?

Notes for parents and carers

Independent reading
The aim of independent reading is to read this book with ease. This series is designed to provide an opportunity for your child to read for pleasure and enjoyment. These notes are written for you to help your child make the most of this book.

About the book
Ruby is a star high jumper who thinks her dreams are shattered after a bad skateboarding accident leaves her with memory loss and a broken leg. Ruby must follow the advice of her doctors and work hard in order to recover. When Ruby decides to think positively, she gets a second chance at achieving her dream.

Before reading
Ask your child why they have selected this book. Look at the title and blurb together. What do they think it will be about? Do they think they will like it?

During reading
Encourage your child to read independently. If they get stuck on a longer word, remind them that they can find syllable chunks that can be sounded out from left to right. They can also read on in the sentence and think about what would make sense.

After reading
Support comprehension by talking about the story. What happened? Then help your child think about the messages in the book that go beyond the story, using the questions on the page opposite. Give your child a chance to respond to the story, asking:
Did you enjoy the story and why? Who was your favourite character? What was your favourite part? What did you expect to happen at the end?

PiLL 03-09-2020

Franklin Watts
First published in Great Britain in 2019
by The Watts Publishing Group

Copyright © The Watts Publishing Group 2019
All rights reserved.

Series Editors: Jackie Hamley, Melanie Palmer and Grace Glendinning
Series Advisors: Dr Sue Bodman and Glen Franklin
Series Designer: Peter Scoulding

A CIP catalogue record for this book is
available from the British Library.

ISBN 978 1 4451 6547 9 (hbk)
ISBN 978 1 4451 6548 6 (pbk)
ISBN 978 1 4451 7036 7 (library ebook)

Printed in China

Franklin Watts
An imprint of
Hachette Children's Group
Part of The Watts Publishing Group
Carmelite House
50 Victoria Embankment
London EC4Y 0DZ

An Hachette UK Company
www.hachette.co.uk

www.franklinwatts.co.uk

FSC
www.fsc.org
MIX
Paper from
responsible sources
FSC® C104740